Sometimes the heart wants what the words can't say

The Prerequisite of Love

YASH SETH

BLUEROSE PUBLISHERS
India | U.K.

Copyright © Yash Seth 2024

All rights reserved by author. No part of this publication may be reproduced, stored in a retrieval system or transmitted in any form or by any means, electronic, mechanical, photocopying, recording or otherwise, without the prior permission of the author. Although every precaution has been taken to verify the accuracy of the information contained herein, the publisher assumes no responsibility for any errors or omissions. No liability is assumed for damages that may result from the use of information contained within.

BlueRose Publishers takes no responsibility for any damages, losses, or liabilities that may arise from the use or misuse of the information, products, or services provided in this publication.

For permissions requests or inquiries regarding this publication, please contact:

BLUEROSE PUBLISHERS
www.BlueRoseONE.com
info@bluerosepublishers.com
+91 8882 898 898
+4407342408967

ISBN: 978-93-6452-852-8

Cover Design: Sadhna Kumari
Typesetting: Pooja Sharma

First Edition: September 2024

The Prerequisite of Love

*To mom, dad, didi, jasmine and the ogs
who held me when no one did.*

Contents

1. Me	1
2. Come to me	3
3. Someone asked me what will I do if I got you	6
4. Story	8
5. Excellence	10
6. She	12
7.	14
8. I cant promise you the stars and the moon	16
9. Aint no sunshine when shes gone	19
10. When a poet met a singer	21
11. Memories	23
12. Late night talks	26
13. Ahh hello my girl	28
14. Ahh my safe spot	30
15. October	32
16.	34
17. Muse	36
18. They say they will do it	38
19. Have you wanted something so bad to lost yourself trying to find it	39

20. I find it weird — 42
21. Bits n pieces — 44
22. Toxic — 46
23. Pain — 48
24. — 51

1. Me

My limelight my heart
My Light has been me
In my depths of uncanny curiosity
I lie with my heart held close
Yet they somehow took that from me
My best sides have been the ones known
In their tranquil life
They have given a light
The light of a dream
Hopefully we can make it ream
Because it's true I live in a dream
In my dreams come my thoughts
In my thoughts comes your face
In my thoughts I sit down
Just to stare as much as I want
For it is she who knows the uncanny curiosity with which I live
With which I love
With which I break
And with that I make
I make myself
I make us
The two who are destined to tear apart
Like a cloth

And all that would remain are the threads
Vulnerable, weak yet hopeful
All those threads would remind me of you
They would remind me of us
In my uncanny curiosity
They questions start with us
And end with how
How do we manage something which we don't have
How do we succeed when we are destined to fail
Yet we try
Ignoring the pries
In the end all that remains is my thoughts
And in them we lie
On a sunny winter morning
Facing each other
Because there would be no thoughts
There would be no destiny
There would only be us.
-yash

2. Come to me

Oh my darling come to me and play

Give me a moment to sway you away

Give me a moment with you

A bit of love in the air

A bit of toxicity in the body

A bit of pain in the eyes

A lot of love in the soul

With it I wait for the moment to become a reality

For you I have all the partiality

For you I do favours

Make you taste different flavours

Flavours of myself

Make you see the colors of you

Make you feel better

Write you letters

Write letters on your body

Make you feel each word as we compose the symphony

With your eyes dripping knowing it is the start of it

It has to be the most beautiful part of it

I know your eyes tell a story

I want to hear them with your lips on mine

I want to feel that taste divine

I want you to revive

For you are my story

My destination

My perception

My bewilderment

My heart

For you have a part of my soul

You have forgiven all my fouls

For you I stay up like a night owl

For it is you who has my bowl

A bowl full of love and passion

A life full of surprises

And a lot of prizes

Of different sizes

I know you and you know yourself

I know you yearn for me

I know you turn for me

I know you learn for me

I know I learn for you

I know I earn for you

I know I live for you

For you are my favourite view

With you the old things feel new

With you the normal feels special

With you I be me

With me you will be you

So come to me

Come to me and feel the story we write

Feel the demons we fight
Feel the light we have
And together we will save
Each other.
-yash.

3. Someone asked me what will I do if I got you

I would look at you and stare
I would walk with you to the places I don't show anyone
On the side walk of a lake I would sit with you and make a pact
To keep us intact
I would hold your hand
Smell your hairband
I would run my hand through your hair
And would know there is nothing more fair
Then the skin which is hidden by the hair
Let the skin feel free
While I admire and look at you with a not so hidden desire
I would desire and look at the fire
Which you hide in your eyes
Make sure that you let it out
With a hand on your neck I would feel it
Hold your hand and then
I would dance with you
I would let the rush prance on you
I would let you feel the feeling what I long to feel
Put my hand on your waist
I would pull you closer
And turn you around

We shall dance in a place not found
I would look into your eyes and smile
For I would know what you would feel
I shall take your hand and make you twirl
And make sure at that moment all the world swirls
Under the stars we shall compose a symphony
A symphony so soothing and exciting at the same time
The ones who don't feel it will not get the rhyme
In that symphony we shall become one
I wish to lock my lips with yours and taste the nectar of you
I wish to care for you
With the passion burning brighter than ever
We shall be what we are
We shall be lovers
And we will have a story
Written with the nectar of you as the ink
I would be standing on the brink
The brink of the terrace with you in my arms
Perhaps euphoria will exist in that moment
There would be nothing else that would matter
At that night the stars will embrace their luck
And the universe will come to a balance
And yet we shall not be in balance
We shall be wild and free
And be whatever we want to be
We shall be one
For that night only but
We shall be one.
 -yash

4. Story

Beneath her glasses lies a world full of story
I would want to know them all
In her glass lies a drink of estacy
I want to drink with her
In her smile lies the heart of many
I want to laugh with her
In her hand lies insecurities of the world
I want to hold her hand
Wear her band
Tie her hair
Touch each layer
Layer of her soul which she hides
In her heart a big secret does reside
In her eyes there is a concern
There is someone for whom she yearns
I yearn for her
I turn for her
I learn for her
I earn for her
For it is her who is in my heart
And every other body part
For it is her who is in my eyes
When I am with her its all smiles

Definitely there will be trails
There will be circumstances
There will be chances
There will be beasts prancing
Our insecurities dancing
But we will work through it
We will ace the test
And together we shall rest
We create a world full of zest
We don't include any pest
We will care about the rest
In that world we will lye
And definitely not lie
If she cries
Ill wipe her tears
If she is scared
Ill take her fears
If she is there
Ill shed my fears
I know of her and I know her
I want to know what lies in her mind
What is it which makes her grind
I don't know much
But there is a force with does make us bind
In her admiration I go blind
For her it is the world she will bind
For me it is her for whom I will grind.
 -yash.

5. Excellence

It has no dependence
It knows no existence
It has no preference
Except you
Without you it feels it is few
Not many
Without you it feels underwhelmed
Perhaps it has succumbed
Succumbed to your soul
Put itself in a bowl
For a meal you can have
And give it the joy of being consumed by you
Idk weather it is true or not
But trust me when excellence sees you tie a knot in your hair
That sight it feels is pretty rare
A sight full of life and delight
A sight full of beauty and glee
Perhaps it is needed
For excellence to realise what it does not have
And yet I do
I have you
Maybe not in person
Maybe not in my life but

In my thoughts
My dreams
My eyes
My laptop and whatever I have
It has you
And trust me you hit me like a flu
I know not what to do
Where to do
How to live
And yet I know it feels good
It feels right
The sight of you feels right
It does reduce all the frights and lessens the fights
It uplifts you
And sure it does hurt
Yet pain never felt good
Maybe it is true
You hit me like a flu.
 -yash

6. She

When I look her into her eyes
All my disdain dies
All our hope says retry
Her eyes showed the story of the universe
Gleamed with glee
All her body said
Why are you like this
We know we are in a constant crisis
We have lived our lives in fear
Why do you want to let anyone near
What if
What if they hear
Eyes replied
If only could someone help with the fear
Then why not hold them dear
The world was my playground
Not my battleground
It's time for an ally
Who makes my troubles go by
To which the ally replied
Our lives have not been lived with fear
But the sad truth is the ones we hold dear
Are often far than near

But
When I look into your soul
It makes my world whole
When I see you smile
I get my reason
And what are we anyway
Fighting the odds or odds fighting us
No one gets it
We try to combine
To live and love inside this porcupine
-yash

7.

It felt true when ramji told sita maa "I don't need the heaven if I cant have you"
And I feel I do would agree to do so too
If I don't have you by my side helping me to brew
Or maybe cook up a new stew
It felt real and surreal
Because it did feel scary
It means it is dreary
Dreary without you
Dreary without the eyes which say a lot
They know how to melt my frost
They know how to clean the dirt
They know ive been hurt
And yet they don't take me for granted
It feels as if something in them is planted
It feels as if it is surreal
And for real it is
It is cute and she is a beaut
It is kind and trust me if I don't see her
I might go blind
I sit here hoping I can help her find
The stars I see in her eyes
Which have burnt and cried

And I looked at them and I lived
For I felt I had been dead
For the first time I felt
And did not have to deal with the consequences dealt.
 -yash

8. I cant promise you the stars and the moon

I can get you flowers though
Feed you with me spoon
Swoon you away from your troubles
Take all your struggles
Make them into bubbles
And fly them away
And then I shall make you sway
Sway you off your feat
I cant promise you the stars and the moon
But I can promise to sit next to you when your world seems to collapse
I can promise to stand by you when you feel your intrusive thoughts will have you relapse
Collapse is what I can do for you
Collapse in order to save you from a relapse
I cant promise you stars and the moon
Yet I can promise to walk with you to any and every place you want to go
Yet I can promise to compromise my Sunday afternoon if you feel doomed
I can promise to get you food
And make sure it tastes good

I cant promise to get you the stars and moon but
I can try to get you jewels
But what will they do
For they will not seem shiny enough infront of your eyes
I can promise to be there
Even if I am seen nowhere I will be there
Somewhere in the dark
Smiling from within knowing you are everything that is right in the universe
I cannot promise you the moon and stars yet
I can promise everything I have written above
So tell me my love
Will you free this dove
Will you take this deal
Will you let me make you feel how I feel
How I feel when I think of you
So lets get this real
You take this deal your world will be surreal
And for real it will have problems and issues
It will have concerns and inconveniences
But it will also have us
So we will negotiate with the issues
When you cry I will hold the tissues
There might be a lot of miss yous'
And if u feel tired I shall be your masseuse
So tell me will you blow this fuse
Or will you be my muse

Will you take this deal
Or let me continue to feel how I feel?
-yash.

9. Aint no sunshine when shes gone

Perhaps she does cast a spell
In which I dwell
With a bundle of blushing I swell
With a tear in my eye I pray
Asking the cost for this person to stay
Asking for opportunities on daily basis
So that I can make her sway
Sway her off her feet
Make her realise she has attained genuine feats
I ask for moments
Moments when I can have her
And smile and delight
Perhaps forget my frights
And be with myself while being with her
It is funny how my words are runny
When i finally speak
And maybe this is what I seek
And trust me when i say this is what we write about
Her thoughts a could around my mind
Making me find perfection
As its an early detection
And if perfection would compare itself to her

It would feel imperfect
It would know it has some defect
It would know what perfection looks like
Maybe one day I will sit with her and we will strike
Strike laughter and jokes
Maybe play with some forks
Create a symphony
And look at the irony
A symphony cant be played
And yet we can
Broken fixing each other we smile
Feeling the romcom feeling
It did leave me reeling
Left me happy
And for the first time left me content.
 -yash.

10. When a poet met a singer

A few words were said
A few rhymes were made
The same old songs were played
Perhaps it was the mutual pain which was being delayed
When a poet met a singer
A few words he wrote
A few verses she sang
As time passed the bell rang
Ting tong said the bell
And both of them were like what the hell
For it was the pain standing at the doorstep
Eating his favourite crepe made from our tears
I mean both of them held it very dear
And while the poet met the singer
He put is phone on silent from ringer
He felt that destiny played its game to bring her
And indeed she knew what she felt
I assume for the first time she was okay with the cards dealt
And then the poet looked into her eyes
No doubt he got butterflies
Despite so many tries he couldn't fight off
And he couldn't write off
He couldn't fight of the blush

That emotional rush
With the touch of his brush he writes what he feels
He sees the singer and in front of her he kneels
For he longs to know what she feels
And now the poet is with the singer
Destiny played its game to bring her
Now his phone is on ringer
And besides his phone he waits
Every moment without her he hates
Both of them have been on a date
And somehow they are the only people who relate
Usually they debate
Many a times they fight
For both of them believe they are right
And at night the ringer rings to his delight
Perhaps that is the time they resort the fight
So now the poet has the singer
And now he feels what should he bring her
Bring her flowers or bring her cakes
Those evening walks they take
Bring her gifts or bring her towers
Perhaps she is the only person he savours not devours
If the tale starts it will last for hours
And that is the story of how the poet met the singer.
 -yash

11. Memories

Here I sit writing listening about hills
Hills take me back to where I began
A place from where I ran
For a better future
To a place where I could be nurtured
And as I come to the end of my school life
I go back to the start of it
Which is the most significant part of it
Which has the heart of it
Which was the start of it
I remember standing and sobbing watching my family depart
That pain became a part
A part of my existence
No matter the resistance
It was a part of my existence
Persistently life went on
I had my firsts there
I learnt the ways of the flirts there
I saw my growth spurts there
I faced my emotions for the first time there
I faced my fears there
And it all felt funny
Except it wasn't

I felt what we call a crush
Which went on to crush my hopes indeed
Which had my emotions going down the slopes indeed
I remember my days and rejoice
And wonder what would have happened had I not made that choice
Would I still rejoice
Would I still suffice
Would I still write
Would I be strong enough to fight my fights
Could it happen that I would not have had to spend my nights
Spend my nights crying or trying
Seems as if the road not taken
Seems as if the question left unanswered
Feels like I have transferred
And acquired the ways of myself
Now I put my memories in a shelf
And hopefully focus on myself
Ironically enough I can't focus on myself
For I sit with the memories and admire
Sadly enough I retire
It is all a comical satire
Now I wear a different attire
Now I speak a different way
Now I wait to hear back
Now I wait to restack my stack
Now I have an attack

An attack of the memories which I had taken for granted
There is not much I can say
Except the fact that they were enchanted
No matter how they were
They were enchanted.
-yash.

12. Late night talks

I talk to the stars about you
my scars found comfort inside you
a smile finds its way to my face when I am with you
it all feels so new and yet it does not
I don't know what good I did that the universe tied this knot
I hope the bond breaks never
Together we shall sit next to a river
And there we will deliver
A laugh
A hug
A moment
The moment of eternity that I wanted would be this
A life of comfort will be this
We both aren't perfect
We both have scars
A variety of cars
Together we will drive them all
A cuisine full of love
I will serve to you
For it is you who heard me and listened to it
For it is you who knew me and knew of me
It gets difficult not to say it
Every moment makes it harder for me

As much as I try not to I cant stop myself from saying it
I cant stop myself from saying the truth
The truth is that I love you
I love you when I make you smile
I love you when you scold me
I love you when the thought of you holds me
I love you when you make me fold inside of me
All this seems different and still it doesn't
All of this seems safe and still it doesn't
For I have my scars and my fears
And they return
I try to give them up
This time I will succeed
This time I will defeat them
For you
For it is you who is my Alby
For it is you who is my partner
It is you who made me restart believing in myself
Now I wish to put your fears on a shelf
And lock them away
For I don't want them coming in our way
For I don't want hinderance while I try to sway you away
Sway you away from yourself
Make you feel safe
Make you feel belonged
Make you mine.
 -yash.

13. Ahh hello my girl

Why aren't you here yet
Why can't you bear it
Why are you always away
Why are u not in my sights
Why do you not take part in my delights
Why are you somewhere
I am looking for you
And I've reached nowhere
I hope to meet you
I hope to greet you
I hope to sit with you and talk
I hope to go out with you and walk
I hope to stand with you and say nothing
Hopefully you'll understand something
I do wish to meet you roz
And maybe greet you with a rose
And then I hope to stay with you
Till time departs
Till both of our times part
And then too shall I be with you
For our souls are aligned
For our life is designed
To suit us

To give us fruits
Fruits of the works we've done
For then shall we become one
In the midst of all this I ask
Why aren't you here yet.
-yash

14. Ahh my safe spot

You know how I've tried not to resort
Resort to you
But every time destiny has something new to brew
I hate it
I love it
I don't know how and why have I come here
I never look at the rear
Rear side of things
My suburban thought has taken a toll
My decisions need a poll
Whether they are right or they be wrong
It's just the feeling in my heart thats so bloody strong
Trust me it's just how it is
It's like a new design
However I feel like I should resign
Resign from being me
For thee would have better plans
For that place would have better plains
For this would be something right
Hopefully my future would be bright
For thee tells me to be me
For this may be a parody
Perhaps it's a fallacy

Perhaps you are a fallacy
But damn it!
My wretched self wants you to be real
It's almost surreal
Losing and winning
With every fall I fall
With every dawn I rise hoping for that call
Hoping for that foe
Somehow she's manages to woe
Woe me to her
Woe me to my thoughts
My disbelief
My hopelessness
Perhaps I have tried
Maybe I have signed
For now all I know is that I have not resgined.
-yash.

15. October

The autumn feeling
Kind of left my heart reeling
And left it crawling
Crawling it came to you
Fixed itself by just looking into your eyes
Your eyes
As if the ocean wasn't deep enough
Somehow pulled me into your not so rough land of dream
And silly me I thought thee had a future to ream
A present we saw
A past we had
A thought we brought
A way you taught
Left the last thought of pain
In the rain
Alas we couldn't be in the rain
And here I find myself sitting in the rain
With my emotions drained
Thoughts refrained
Picking up pieces of what had come crawling to you
We thought we could brew

Perhaps a new stew
A new thought
The thought I have
Is present
And so are you
But not together
I thought of meeting you on the 3rd of December
Hopefully we have a time to remember
I showed everything and I regret
Perhaps its true
Love hits like a flu
Like a cool breeze during the summer loo
Admist all this I have a thought to brew
Perhaps renew
Maybe cook another stew
Start another story
This time leading to glory.
 -yash.

16.

A song

A place

A memory

It doesn't go does it?

Still reminds of the place where you were left you at your worst

Well wait for some time it'll get better

They will realise what they lost

Who they left in the frost

Remember the close ones

For they are the only ones who

Will be happy for you

Make you believe to try for something new

And remember it is not your safe space

It is your escape and scape

It is your landscape and is your plaintiff

Make sure to not fall of the cliff

Make sure you don't get frantic

While looking down the cliff

It looks good from afar

Make sure you reach that star

And flaunt that scar

Take that car

And be the star

Spread light
Be bright
Spread your love
Be the go getter
Make things better
And then you shall get what u deserve
You will get peace.
 -yash.

17. Muse

I remember the time when I didn't write
And yet I had let myself loose
And yes you have blown my fuse
For I had given everything and you didn't want it
Toxicity is what you wanted
And if that's what you want it is what you shall get
And yet the person you want will try to strangle your neck
Make sure you don't peck
Peck of his plate
So you might as well live with it
But remember it has no worth
Because remember that your life will have no dearth
And you will roam this earth
With a sense of fear
For the one you hold near
Is the person keeping you rear
Keeping you on the rear seat of your life
How is this a life
How will you survive
And it is all so funny
For you I had my tears runny
For you I had my life lost
For you I was always stuck

For you I had given my everything
For you I was left stranded
For you I had waited
Just to receive 'I am sorry'
But the truth is you are not
You never wanted to tie the knot
And I had been made to think that you hoped to tie the knot
'maybe this is what true love feels like'
This is not what love feels like
Remember you are a great person
And yet you chose to do what was wrong for you
So you might as well go on and be happy
For I am done with thinking of you
And making my life scrappy
Before going answer me
Did that night mean nothing to you
And if it didn't
Then why did you choose to show that it did
For I know I wasn't the one you wanted
And you were the one I needed
Despite knowing that you lead on
Cooked me into a prawn
And threw me away
And silly me I thought you were making me sway
Yet I continued
I shall not do it anymore.
  -yash.

18. They say they will do it

But they never do
I guess this is what adulting feels like
When the blood of the Covent leaves
Its stains of you on you
When the Covent bleeds you dry
And you live lifelessly
I will not adult this way.

19. Have you wanted something so bad to lost yourself trying to find it

And yes you did get it
Only for a while
It did leave a smile when you had it in your arms
And then came the storms
Which took it away
You kept looking at it
While it flew over your head into the arms of someone else
It is a different kind of stress
Knowing it is not right and yet it is
Knowing it is not believable
And yet it is
It is a different story
Perhaps you didn't know it
Perhaps you didn't know what it meant
To live with the cards I had been dealt
You forgot the emotions you felt and flew away with the storm
And like everything else you broke into this norm
The norm to be human
Amidst all this I realised I cant have you
And yes it is alright

It is a different fight
It is something where I am not involved
Although I am dissolved
Dissolved into your thought
The memories you had brought
Dissolved into being yours even if you aren't mine
This feeling is sublime
It does leave me reeling
And for sure it helps the feeling
Feeling of belief
Belief that someday someone will be mine
And the truth is I am already on cloud nine
Because your mare thought is so fine
It leaves me trying to make you mine
And I might be able to do it
I may not
But yes I will tie the knot
Knot to what I feel
Knot to how I deal with what I feel
Knot which makes me reel
Reel under your pressure
Reel under your smile
Reel under your eyes
Make you some fries
And maybe have other tries
Too much of me gets the better of me
And yet you get the best of me

And yes you get the best of what I am
Trust me this is not a scam
You get the best of what I am.
 -yash

20. I find it weird

That ive started to write a lot
A few demons inside me head say ive started to fight a lot
A voice in my head says I delight more often
Feels like my rock hard heart has been softened
Feels like the frost has started to melt
Maybe I am enjoying the cards that ive been delt
Maybe I have accepted myself
Maybe I have rejected myself
And yet I look back at the dejected self and I smile
Because I know that just lasted for a while
You just lasted for a while
Meanwhile i fixed myself to be better
And gathered some courage to send the letter
At that time my words were tested
Emotions felt unrested for you had disappeared
And left me hanging
Sitting in the balcony on the cold night I thought
Is this frost just outside or does it have its roots in me
All this while I felt myself weaken and soften
For the deepest-rooted insecurities had come alive
And they had started to thrive
For I know I was alone
But for the first time I felt lone

For I know I had been left hanging
But for the first time I felt the pain of it
For I know I was nothing
But for the first time I felt nothing
No wonder they say love hurts and heals
It closes all those deals
Which weren't meant to be closed
This isn't how it was supposed to be posed
All this I was and yet this is all I am
In my entirety calm
In my thoughts happy
For I have accepted I may not have you
But you exist
I may not get you
But you get me
I may not be what I am
But you are all I would want to be
In this world of shackles you are free
To be honest you are all I would want to be.
 -yash.

21. Bits n pieces

Everytime I see you my heart seizes
For I know you have shattered it into bits n pieces
And my heart seizes
I see you and delight
For I know I have another fight to fight
Another room to light
Perhaps your room has been lit up
And yes you have been lit up
And yet trying to light you up
I lost my light
My delight
My strength to fight
My immune to reside
And my will to write
Admits all this I find myself to be thinking
While I find myself drinking
That what did I do wrong
Why did I choose not to be strong
Why I did I let myself loose
And most of all why did you use
Use the light that I had
And leave none for me
Use all the delights that I had

And leave none for me
Use all the life I had
And leave none for me
I mean its funny
How my tears are always so runny
And yet they don't run
For they know watching them fall would give you the fun
The fun to watch someone kneel and knel
To watch someone cry and pry
To watch them create a hue and cry
To watch them do the dance of misery
How merciless do you have to be
With someone you had a history
With someone who died
While you watched his emotions fried
Tears dried
Words tried
And yet nothing happened.
  --yash

22. Toxic

It is a feeling so exotic
A sensation so good
A rush so fast
That you forget the spells it does cast
A feeling exotic enough
To make you lose your senses
To make you do those dances
Dances of misery and pain
Of discomfort and disdain
To make you believe in the unbelievable
To make you question the inevitable
What it meant was such
That you will never know much
Much of what they do
Much of what they try to do
It is a different story on how they grew
Grew into this person who harms and breaks
Knows you don't know how to take
Take the feeling of being stranded
They know you feel stranded
They know and they understand
And that is why you don't deserve a chance
A chance to stand against them

A chance to stand for yourself
Because they function in a different realm
You never know what to expect
How to detect and how to accept
Accept that youre being taken for granted
Because you that feeling is so enchanted
An enchanted feeling
Which leaves you reeling
Leaves you crumbling and somewhat fumbling
Leaves you stranded.
 -yash

23. Pain

Quite a lovely feeling isn't it
Makes you bow down doesn't it
Makes you disbelief yourself
And why shouldn't it
You've grown up with fire
It is a comical satire
A unique mystery
Which leads nothing but misery
A unique dichotomy
Makes all the things look stormy
Except the storm itself
Sets a few norms for itself
To escape the storm you look for distractions
Some instant satisfaction
But the truth is the storm is you
In the darkest coffee that you brew
You forgot to realise that the storm was in you
A burning desire
Makes your satire looks real
Which makes your real looks boring
Gives you the rush
Makes you shush
Puts you into your place

Tells you not to run this race
And puts you to your knees
Gets you out of contact with yourself
Gets you into your head
Makes the green look red
And vice versa
Its true that loves made you crazy
And if it doesn't it isn't alright
But you should choose to fight your fight
Realise your right
And yet there is pain
A feeling so satirical
It makes you beg on your knees to stay
Allows you to look for opportunities to sway
Sway yourself away from you
Makes you jump into the pot of stew
And makes you come out a new
Burnt and well done
Then you realise you don't answer to none
And yet you look for that one
who can make you feel what you've always felt
Makes you want to fold the cards you've dealt
It is a drug
Makes you a thug
Makes you beg
A comical addiction
Which gives you a painful satisfaction

A forbidden desire
And yes an unexplainable satire.
 -yash.

24.

Perhaps this situation has ended
Perhaps we have ended
With not so subtle scars
And maybe some fault in our stars
We have ended
Though the hopes remain
Still sits on the same train
Though the belief stayed
It is also true that scars hurt
They make sure I suffer
Make me feel like I'm a duffer
A duffer I am
A knobhead I was
For once I believed life is a comedy
And it did prove to be one
However I was the mockery and the situation a joke
All we can do is sit down and laugh
Maybe someday we'll sit in another bus
With different lives
Maybe we won't have have the same lives
But we would have the same eyes
Perhaps this situation has ended
But my heart chooses not to believe

Perhaps I am running down a hopeless drain
Sometimes I think I shouldve reconsidered boarding the train
Maybe someday we'll meet up
And i get another chance to rizz up
Hopefully we will
For now I stay with a not so subtle scar
A lot of pain in my heart
Assuming there was some fault in the stars
-yash

www.ingramcontent.com/pod-product-compliance
Lightning Source LLC
LaVergne TN
LVHW041635070526
838199LV00052B/3369